For Sally
J.C.

For Liz
C.V.

First published 1995 by Walker Books Ltd
87 Vauxhall Walk, London SE11 5HJ

This edition published 1996

10 9 8 7 6 5 4 3 2

Text © 1995 June Crebbin
Illustrations © 1995 Clara Vulliamy

This book has been typeset in Monotype Baskerville.

Printed in Hong Kong

British Library Cataloguing in Publication Data
A catalogue record for this book is
available from the British Library.

ISBN 0-7445-4371-1

Danny's Duck

June Crebbin

Illustrated by
Clara Vulliamy

WALKER BOOKS
AND SUBSIDIARIES
LONDON • BOSTON • SYDNEY

A duck flew over the land,
looking for a good woody place.
Down she flew to a pile of brushwood
at the edge of a school playground.

No one saw her come.

Except Danny.

At playtime he looked for her.
He had to look hard. Her colours
were so like the colours of the twigs
and branches. But Danny saw her.

And she saw him.

In school Danny drew the duck sitting.

"How lovely," said his teacher. "A duck on her nest."

When Danny visited the pile of
brushwood again, the duck was still there,
sitting very still. Again she saw him.
Then she stood up and stretched.

Danny saw her eggs.
He looked and counted.

In school he drew a picture of the nest
with nine pale green eggs in it.

"How lovely," said his teacher.
"They'll have ducklings inside, growing."

Danny visited the duck every day.
Children played in the playground.
Parents passed close by on the footpath.
But no one saw.

One sunny morning, just as he always did,
Danny ran into the playground and over
to the pile of brushwood.

But the duck wasn't there.
Nor were her eggs.
The nest was empty.

Danny cried.
He cried and cried.

In school he drew a picture of the empty nest.
But when his teacher saw the picture – she smiled!

"The mother duck eats the egg-shells," she said,
"after the eggs have hatched."

At lunch-time, Danny took his teacher
across the playground to the pile of brushwood.

There was the nest.

Then his teacher took Danny
across the school field, to the pond.

Danny looked.

"There's my duck!" he shouted.
"And – one, two, three, four, five,
six, seven, eight, *nine ducklings*!"

And everyone came to see.

MORE WALKER PAPERBACKS
For You to Enjoy

ELLEN AND PENGUIN
by Clara Vulliamy

Ellen is small and shy. So is her soft-toy penguin.
But, as they discover at the park, they are not the only ones.

"This is a delightful story which should help anxious and emotionally
insecure children to feel less isolated." *Child Education*

0-7445-3658-8   £4.50

FLY BY NIGHT
by June Crebbin/Stephen Lambert

All day long a young owl, Blink, sits on his branch,
waiting impatiently to take flight for the very first time.
The wood about him is full of activity.
But when will *his* moment come?

"A rich introduction to what a good story
is all about – perfect for reading aloud and relishing
the pictures." *Children's Books of the Year*

0-7445-3627-8   £4.50

THE TRAIN RIDE
by June Crebbin/Stephen Lambert

Told in simple, rhythmic sentences with a repeated refrain
and dazzling pictures, this account of a little girl's train journey
takes the reader along for the ride too!

0-7445-4701-6   £4.99